Welcome to the Pit!

The underground headquarters of the G.I. Joe Team is your new home. That's because you are about to become their newest member.

Your Code Name: Dog Ear.

Your major talents: Brainy and street-smart, you know how to fight and how to fly a plane.

Your assignment: Intelligence.

As a member of the G.I. Joe Team, you are expected to pull your weight, even if it is your first mission. You are being counted on to use your skills in a perfect blend of thought and action.

You will be asked to make many crucial decisions. After you do, follow the directions at the bottom of each page.

If you make the right decisions, the team will triumph over the evil forces of COBRA, and you will be a hero. If you make the wrong choices, your first mission may be your last.

Good luck, Dog Ear. Your mission begins on page 1.

Other G.I. JOE_{TM} books in
the FIND YOUR FATE_{TM} series
Published by Ballantine Books:

G.I. JOE

OPERATION: TERROR TRAP

BY H. WILLIAM STINE AND
MEGAN STINE

BALLANTINE BOOKS • NEW YORK

RLI: $\dfrac{\text{VL Grades 5 + up}}{\text{IL Grades 6 + up}}$

Library of Congress Catalog Card Number: 85-90757

ISBN 0-345-32667-9

Interior design by Gene Siegel
Editorial Services by Parachute Press, Inc.

Manufactured in the United States of America

First Edition: November 1985

Cover Illustration by Carl Cassler
Illustrated by David Henderson

FIND YOUR FATE™*

#4

G.I.JOE

OPERATION: TERROR TRAP

It's so quiet in the central corridor of the second level of the Pit that you can hear your steps echoing—not to mention the beating of your heart! The hand you reach toward the door of the briefing room is sweaty. But you're as ready as you're going to get. You've got your secret arsenal hidden in your shoe and your nerves are steeled. You take a deep breath and...

"Have a seat. We're waiting for you." The tall, cool commander, Hawk, is standing on the briefing stage in front of a large map.

You blush. Are you late? Have you messed up already?

No. "Welcome to the team," Hawk is saying. You turn and look at the others around you. *Your* team!

"Duke here will be in charge," Hawk continues. The blond infantryman reaches over and shakes your hand. You smile, trying to hide a grimace of pain. You're not even going to get past handshaking!

Lady Jaye flashes you a smile. The Lady is tops in intelligence. To work with her is a terrific bonus!

"Lady Jaye, Dog Ear, and Quick Kick, who's already on his way to the site, will do the scouting," says Hawk. "Duke, Dusty, and Gung-Ho are backup."

You admire Dusty's Lawrence-of-Arabia uniform as he gives you the thumbs-up sign.

Turn to page 2.

"Welcome, *mon cha*," says Gung-Ho.

"That means 'my dear' in Cajun," Lady Jaye whispers in your ear. Your eyes almost pop. The toughest Marine in the world just called you "my dear"! Then you look at the scowl behind Hawk's smile as he begins to explain the mission, and you sit up straighter.

A picture of a real weirdo is flashed on the screen. His coal-black hair looks unreal above a pale face with piercing black eyes. His sweeping black robe is decorated with feathers, beads, shells, and a necklace of tiny skulls.

"Do we have to bring him back to life?" asks Lady Jaye without cracking a smile.

"This guy for real?" says Dusty, astounded that anyone prefers black to sand, his favorite color.

"I'm afraid so," answers Hawk. "He calls himself The One. He's carved out a country for himself in North Africa. Calls it Kamali. Did it quick and dirty, grabbing it without a 'please' or 'thank you.' In one month he's overpowered the troops of the neighboring country of Mombania, and built a modern capital—Kamali City—complete with a castle! The guy's no slouch.

"We don't think he's working alone. His takeover was too fast for that. Maybe the Russians are behind it, but they don't like to see their puppets living the high life. More likely, the power behind The One is COBRA!"

....

Go on to page 3.

Lady Jaye speaks. "Our mission is to infiltrate Kamali, discover The One's plans, and give him the old heave-ho. The One is really Parker Shaw of the Bronx, New York. Seems he was a real-estate tycoon who found the U.S. confining. Wanted a country of his own. His headquarters are in an old mansion in Westchester County, north of New York City. This may also be a recruiting station. If COBRA is behind The One, he's too close for comfort."

Right, you think. Less than fifty miles from the Pit!

"Dog Ear," Hawk is saying, "Quick Kick is at Grand Central Terminal right now, about to take a train to Westchester."

"A train!" Gung-Ho exclaims.

"Surveillance of The One's HQ must be under *very* deep cover," says Hawk. "What could be better than something so normal—the train, a rental car, nothing out of the ordinary. The rest of the team is going straight to Kamali. Which would you rather do, Dog Ear?"

· ·

If you decide to join Quick Kick at Grand Central and investigate The One stateside, turn to page 17.

If you decide to go straight to Africa with the rest of the team, turn to page 66.

The pick! That's it!

You look out of your cell down the corridor to make sure no one's coming, then slip the pick out of its hiding place in the heel of your shoe.

There's not much light in here. But you've practiced this blindfolded in training. You can do it by touch.

You trace the lock with your fingers. Insert the pick. Careful now, ease it, don't rush, this is delicate.

There! You hear it start to slide. It makes a little tick and...

And...oh, no! You forgot a basic rule of training. You didn't check for a tamper-proof device.

Too bad, Joe.

Your carelessness just—*KAPOW*—blew you away!

THE END

"We've got to save Gung-Ho!" Lady Jaye insists.

Dusty sees that the Lady is going to have her way. "Grab his feet!" he yells at you.

Gung-Ho is 250 pounds of dead weight. And worse, the bodyguards are rushing at you, followed by the palace guards brandishing those needles again. *What* is going on here?

"Oooof!" Lady Jaye exclaims. "That stings!"

"Ow!" grunts Dusty.

You can't see what's happening because Gung-Ho's huge, limp body is in front of you like a shelf. Then a palace guard rushes up on your left and pops you with a needle.

You drop Gung-Ho. Something very strange is happening. All your energy and bravery are disappearing. You start to tremble...to quiver ...to cry. You are *scared to death*! You want to go somewhere and pull the covers over your head.

Your wish is granted. The four of you, sobbing and sniveling, are led out across the courtyard to a barracks. You crawl into a narrow bed and pull up the covers. But what if something's *under* the bed?

You're too scared to look. You jam your pillow over your head. What will happen? Are you going to rot here?

Is whatever was in those needles the secret of The One's power? Did Duke escape and call for help? You'll never know. You're much too scared to ask.

THE END

5

COBRA Commander nods as the two guards finish their work. "I do hope you boys like to visit foreign cities," he says. "What I have in mind for you two is—"

But before he can finish, Quick Kick goes into action. COBRA Commander has made a small mistake. He has had Quick Kick's hands tied—but not his legs! With one lightning-swift motion, Quick Kick spins around and kicks the weapon from one of the guards' hands.

"*Stop!*" COBRA Commander screams.

You realize you have only a split second to act!

Turn to page 37.

"We don't stand a chance against a whole COBRA battalion!" you scream. "Let's get back to the plane!"

The five of you, ducking low as the weapon fire roars over your heads, turn and run back down the ridge, struggling to keep your balance on the rocky cliffs. COBRAS, on foot, are right behind you.

Soon the path becomes steeper as you climb back toward the landing strip. You turn and look down. The COBRAS are gaining on you. The landing strip comes into view. The plane awaits.

Can you reach it and get away before the COBRAS catch up and capture you?

Your teammates are several yards ahead of you. You run as hard as you can, trying to catch up. Suddenly, you trip. You fall. You roll down a hot sand gully.

"Dog Ear—get up! Hurry!" Lady Jaye calls from way up ahead.

You struggle to your feet, stumble, get up again, and run toward the plane. Its engines roar to life. The plane is about to take off.

COBRA soldiers are closing in. They stop and set up their weapons, preparing to blast the plane.

The plane slowly moves down the runway. You run faster, faster.... Will it take off without you?

Turn to page 80.

You've got to stand and fight. Otherwise, none of you will make it!

AACCKKK AACCKKK AACCKKK! Three short blasts from your automatic pistol, and another three guards fall.

"Don't wait for me, gentlemen," Lady Jaye snorts and then punctures daylight through three more with her M-16.

You're doing great when—holy cow!—more guards crash in. But—*KAPLOW*—so does Duke, fresh from victory in the courtyard!

"Hit 'em again, guys!" shouts Duke.

They're doing just fine, but your mission will be for nothing unless you can get The One out of here alive! But where is he? You peer through the smoke and bullets and spy him hiding under his desk!

You make a dive for The One and press your machine pistol against his head.

"Hold it!" The One shouts to his guards. "Lay down your weapons!"

"That's right," you yell, "unless you want to see your fearless leader turned into a pattern on the wallpaper!"

Go on to page 9.

"Don't kill me," begs The One, "and I'll tell you what's wrong with your friend."

Your friend?

Gee, you'd almost forgotten all about Gung-Ho. He's crying like a baby in the corner.

The guards frown and grumble, but follow The One's orders and leave you all alone for a powwow.

"Your big friend here," says The One, pointing at Gung-Ho, "has been injected with poltron, a fantastic substance found only in the ore here in Kamali mines. It turns the bravest soldier into a sniveling coward!"

"So *that's* what's wrong with him," says Lady Jaye. "Poor thing."

"And," continues The One, "do you see what a marvelous weapon it is? I turned the entire country of Mombanians, whose land the mines were on, into frightened children."

"So that is how you got your own country," Duke says.

"Well, I'd always wanted one." The One smiles.

"So why haven't you lived happily ever after?" you ask sarcastically.

"Because COBRA Commander and his pals heard about poltron and moved right in on your little empire, right?" Duke says.

The One nods feebly.

....
Turn to page 87.

9

"What do you think is waiting for us down there?" you ask Lady Jaye as the chopper hovers over The One's palace.

She looks down. "Just five guards. They're expecting this copter back anyway. Okay, guys, what's the plan?"

"Five guards!" snorts Gung-Ho. "That's one apiece. Hardly worth working up a sweat for. Can I have two?"

"Dog Ear and Gung-Ho will penetrate the palace while we clean up the courtyard. Then we'll follow," says Duke. "Ready?"

Lady Jaye leans out the chopper door with her crossbow and fires. "Got mine. Oh, and yours, too, Dusty."

"Dag nab it, Lady Jaye," says Gung-Ho. "Now look what you've done." Six more guards run out of the palace.

Rat-a-tat-tat. Their fire sounds like stirred-up hornets. Quickly Gung-Ho sits the bird down and Lady Jaye, Dusty, and Duke disappear in a blaze of gunfire.

You and Gung-Ho creep toward the palace door, then race down a winding corridor, flinging open doors. Your machine pistols are at the ready. There it is! The One's private office. He's barking orders into a phone. You each grab a bodyguard, but too late. The palace guard charges in, armed with—*needles!?!*

Turn to page 21.

11

The car rental office is across from the train station in the small Westchester village where you get off.

This feels so silly, just renting a car as if you were tourists, but you keep remembering that Hawk said "deep cover." You're supposed to look like ordinary folks.

But Quick Kick doesn't exactly fit that description. The pipe-smoking man behind the rental counter is staring at him.

"I am a guide and interpreter for Mr. How," you say. "He's a very important dignitary up from Washington."

"Yes, sir," the clerk says as he hands you the keys. You don't see him dialing the phone as you drive off.

The road winds for several miles through the countryside and suddenly off to the right is a dead end. And there it is—a huge, rusty iron gate. It isn't even locked.

Once you walk through the gate you see an eerie boarded-up old mansion. Its shutters creak in the wind. It gives you the shivers.

"I think I've seen this place in an old horror movie," you say.

"Things are never as scary as they seem on the outside," Quick Kick replies.

Easy for him to say.

Turn to page 41.

You thank the pizza man—who smiles at you, not skipping a beat of his song—and stand up.

Bad move! The retreating footsteps must have belonged to someone else. Bulldog is standing right in front of you.

"Pepperoni or plain?" you ask as you shove a piping-hot tray in his face and run.

Turn to page 64.

Your hands grasp for the barrel of the blasting machine gun—*and you miss!*

You grab the COBRA around the legs on your way down and pull him to the ground. "Good tackle, Dog Ear!" Dusty cries, finishing the COBRA off. "Looks like it's fourth down for COBRA—and they've got to punt!"

The fight is over, and you have won. Two COBRAS flee across the sand as the rain begins. You laugh, watching them trip and stumble in their long robes. But your celebration is cut short by a loud beeping sound.

"It's coming from the saddlebags on their donkey," Lady Jaye quickly figures out. She runs over to the saddlebags and pulls out a radio receiver.

The beeps continue, a coded transmission. Lady Jaye works to decode the message. The rain stops as suddenly as it started. The sky brightens again. "I've got it!" she cries triumphantly.

"What's the word?" Duke asks seriously.

"I couldn't get a lot of it," she says. "But I got enough to learn that COBRA *has* infiltrated The One's operation—and that something big is about to happen!"

"Let's get moving," Duke says. "Dusty, can you get a fix on our location?"

"By my figuring, Kamali City is a short hike over that ridge," Dusty says.

"I hope you're right," Duke says, as you head toward the ridge. "I've had enough surprises for one day!"

....

Turn to page 74.

14

"We've got to radio our base immediately," Quick Kick says. "Is there a communications room in this place?"

"Wait!" says Lady Jaye. "I don't think we want to radio from here! The place is crawling with guards—and they might monitor all the transmissions. Let's get back to the palace and radio from there. I've got my communicator stashed just outside the palace walls."

"There isn't time! We've got to act now!" Quick Kick insists. "Besides, the palace isn't exactly a safe spot either."

You know they're both right—the situation is tough. It's up to you to make the decision. Decide now!

If you think you should radio from the communications room here at the plant, turn to page 71.

If you think you should return to the palace and radio from there, turn to page 29.

"I just can't make it, Quick Kick," you say.

"Come on," he says. "This is our only chance."

"I know. But I'll just slow you down. Make your break for freedom. Maybe you can come back and get me."

He looks sadly over his shoulder at you and then takes a deep breath and *KAPLOW*! One kick and the door is gone.

You hear him running. Then you hear the *whiz whiz* of bullets. Did they find their target? You're almost too tired to care. You must sleep.

"Ah hah, my little friend. Lying down on the job?" Is this a dream, or is a very tall man with a lightning bolt sticking out of each ear standing over you? "We will begin."

Guards drag your limp body out of the small room and down a corridor to a locked door.

"Here we are," the tall man says. "My office."

Some office, you think, with a big chair with lots of straps and a helmet like a hair dryer in a beauty shop.

It's *your* head that's going to be dried—or fried.

When they start in on you, you have no idea what they're up to. But in a few days, just before your mind has reached the place where COBRA controls it, you're sure you're being brainwashed. A few more days and you have no memory of your former life. You are COBRA!

....

Turn to page 62.

Leaving the Pit behind, you drive to the Staten Island Ferry. The clifflike buildings of Manhattan loom up across the water. You wonder what awaits you beyond them.

It's a little disappointing to begin this mission by dropping your token into a subway turnstile—but you understand the need for deep cover. Well, nothing could be deeper than the subway to Grand Central.

You don't see Quick Kick at the station, so you sit down on a hard bench to wait. Suddenly a fight breaks out between two men in front of you.

ZAP! SNAP! POP! Even though this isn't your Joe mission, you can't just stand by and watch a big bully give it to this little guy on the chin. You've got to get involved.

You reach out for the bruiser, when suddenly from behind you feel someone's eyes on you. You whirl. Quick Kick?

No. You're staring straight into the face of a bulldog of a guy wearing dark glasses and a dark green storm coat. You look away, but too late. He knows you saw him tailing you.

Quick! You have to decide!

....

If you let this bulldog guy shadow you, turn to page 52.

If you try to get him off your scent, turn to page 63.

The plane taxis in for a landing. It comes to a halt. You listen carefully for any clues as to what's happening.

Zzzzzzzzz. What is that? Could someone be snoring?

Then outside, footsteps.

"We can unload them now," says a gruff voice. Light filters in. You close your eyes. Better play possum.

Hands grab you and toss you over someone's shoulder like a sack of potatoes. You open one eye just a bit, enough to see the edge of a COBRA uniform. It all comes back to you.

Where have they taken you? It's someplace hot and dusty. The musical accents of the workers sound African. Has COBRA taken you to Kamali—to The One's little kingdom? It's possible. But you can't know for sure.

Kerplunk. You're dumped in the back of a trunk.

Ooof! Another sack of potatoes. You sneak an eye open. It's Quick Kick—still out like a light. Or is he dead?

Go on to page 19.

You're afraid to find out. But before you have time to think about it, a nudge in your ribs answers the question.

"Shhhhh," Quick Kick cautions you. You wink to let him know you're okay.

In a matter of minutes your journey is over. Still playing possum, you're both lugged off the truck and dropped in a small, windowless room. You *feel* like a sack of potatoes. Dull, with no energy.

"Now?" you whisper.

"Now," he answers. "Let's just hope this dump isn't bugged."

"Where are we? And what are we going to do?" You feel so bad that you hope whatever he has up his sleeve doesn't require much effort on your part.

"We're in Kamali—I heard that from one of the guards. And I don't know about you, but I'm busting out of here *now*. I've had enough free travel, courtesy of COBRA, to last me a lifetime," Quick Kick says.

You watch as he breaks his bonds and draws a lock pick from his shoe. You have to make a decision.

....

Are you going to try to rally and break out with him? If so, turn to page 61.

Or are you just too weak to go on? Would you hold him back? If so, gather your strength on page 16.

19

Remembering your training, you hit the deck, slithering under the guards' feet toward an escape. Almost out, you turn back toward the sound of Gung-Ho's grunting and—

Where's Gung-Ho? Is that him in a corner?

CRASH! The door disappears, its splinters followed by Dusty's fist and Lady Jaye's rifle.

Guards race toward them.

"Let's go, Gung-Ho!" shouts Duke.

But Gung-Ho is rolled up into a little ball in the corner, his hands in front of his face.

"What's wrong with Gung-Ho?" shouts Lady Jaye. "We've got to get him out of here! He's in no shape to protect himself."

"We can't," Dusty disagrees. "These guys are coming right at us. Fight!" He braces himself, ready to roll heads.

What do you do?

....

If you think you should grab the cowering, quivering Gung-Ho and try to escape, turn to page 5.

Is taking a stand now, and worrying about Gung-Ho later, your only hope? If so, turn to page 8.

You decide to take a little while to make a plan. You know that you can break out anytime you want to. At least that's what you tell yourselves.

"I could just kick the bars in," says Quick Kick.

"Too much noise. The guards will come."

"So what do you think?"

You hesitate. After all, *he's* the senior member of the team.

"What if we use my laser knife here," you say, pulling it out of your shoe, "and quietly saw our way through?"

Quick Kick smiles. "Go to it," he says, "but how about sawing these ropes first?"

In no time, Quick Kick is loose and so are the bars.

"Move it," Quick Kick whispers.

You cautiously put one foot out into the corridor—the first step toward freedom.

Turn to page 24.

You run to the left. There's a long hallway— and no one in sight! At the end is a steel door.

SLAM! KERPLOW! Quick Kick's kick breaks it down and you're outside now. You keep running until you hear a husky voice shout, "Stop right there!"

You look up and almost run right into Roadblock. With him are several other members of the team. You recognize Flint and Mutt. Behind them is a whole platoon of regular army troops.

"We figured there was a problem when you didn't report in," Flint says. "So Hawk sent us as a backup team."

You quickly explain that COBRA Commander is in the mansion.

That's all Roadblock has to hear! The G.I. Joe Team storms the place—lobbing tear gas canisters through the windows. COBRA troops answer the fire. But they are no match for G.I. Joe.

Unfortunately, COBRA Commander is not in the mansion after all. He must have slipped away in the middle of the battle. "Don't worry, we'll get that slime another day," says Flint.

You smile; it's good to know there will be another day. Another day to investigate The One and his strange rise to power. Another day for adventure and excitement as you find your fate as a real member of the G.I. Joe Team.

THE END

It's deathly quiet in the corridors. You keep waiting for the sound of running footsteps.

"No silent alarm," whispers Quick Kick. "And no video." He raises his eyebrows in surprise. Maybe COBRA isn't as sophisticated as you'd both thought.

Have the COBRAS all been put out of their misery by a backup Joe Team? Or is this a trick? Are they following you back to the Joe Team, hoping to wipe you all out at once?

"Don't worry, just move!" says Quick Kick. You run! You're outside the mansion now, working your way carefully through the undergrowth of twisted, thorny plants. No one is at the gate. It's eerie.

"What are you doing?" you ask Quick Kick, who's standing in the road with his thumb in the air.

When a truck stops for you, you can't believe it, and neither can the truckdriver when he gets a good look at Quick Kick—who just doesn't look like your average suburbanite.

"Where can I drop you?" the trucker asks respectfully.

"Town, please," Quick Kick answers, "and step on it."

You jerk back against your seat as he takes Quick Kick at his word. In two minutes, you're in a phone booth dialing the G.I. Joe Team's top-secret code number.

"Hold on, we'll be there in a flash," says Hawk.

Turn to page 44.

24

You ask for a private meeting with The One and tell him what you know about the assassination. In return, he tells you why COBRA is so interested in Kamali.

"There are these mines," he tells you, "which is why I came here in the first place. A new ore, called poltron, was discovered. When you process it and combine it with several other chemicals, it has some very interesting properties. It can be injected into a person or inhaled as a gas—and it turns the toughest soldier into a whimpering coward.

"And now COBRA has taken over everything here. I'm not surprised they're planning to do me in. There's something big going on down at the poltron processing plant. And there's a meeting today—COBRA Commander, the Baroness, and Destro. They don't want me anymore. They've stopped asking me to their meetings." The One sounds sorry for himself.

"Listen," you remind him, "they *want* you—dead!"

You've got to find out what COBRA is up to. It's not good news that the Baroness is here. She's as clever as she is vicious. And Destro, the weapons supplier—wouldn't he just love to get a hold of poltron! What's your next move?

....

If you decide to check out the poltron plant, turn to page 34.

If you decide you'd like to sneak into the COBRA meeting, turn to page 54.

25

No, it's not the end. Not yet.

Sometime later—hours, days, months—you start to flicker back to life. Your mind is very dim. You feel as if you have a 15-watt bulb for a brain.

You can't see anything. Are you blind?

No, there's the tiniest crack of light.

You're in a place that's very, very dark.

And you're moving. No, that's not right. You're not moving—you're tied with what feel like thick ropes.

But the dark room you're in is moving.

Suddenly your ears pop. *Ow!* But at least the pain proves you're alive.

What is that noise? That vaguely familiar whine? An airplane! That's what it is—and the pop of your ears means you're landing.

Bump! Bump! Not such a smooth landing, but who cares? You're alive! At least for now!

Turn to page 18.

It's not that you're cowards. But these shop-keepers and merchants in the marketplace have been very nice to you. You'd hate to see your blood and theirs ruining their carpets. So you raise your hands and march.

The fort is a joke. You could break out of it in a second. But you all go along and let the soldiers lock you up in individual cells.

"Things are probably pretty quiet around here," says Duke. The walls are so thin, you can hear each other perfectly. "More guests today than they've seen all year."

As soon as you're settled in, Lady Jaye says, "Quiet! Listen! What's that?"

Sure enough, it's the whir of a helicopter. Coming to take you—where? The palace at Kamali? The bottom of a deep ravine somewhere?

"One chopper can hold all of us," Duke is saying. "Gung-Ho, pop out of that tin can of a cell, and then hide at the end of the corridor in the dark. We'll blow this rinky-dink jail, grab the chopper, and be up, up, and away!"

Turn to page 28.

Two guards unlock the outer door to the cell block and start down the corridor, talking. They don't even see Gung-Ho coming.

His fist makes contact with the speed of a bullet and the force of a bulldozer. *BAP. CRUNCH.* And it's all over.

Pop. Pop. Pop. Pop. Four quick slams and the rest of your cell doors swing open.

"Thank you, Gung-Ho," says Lady Jaye, and he bows graciously.

Outside the cell block door, Gung-Ho, Dusty, and Duke quickly "borrow" the weapons from the dozing guards. Then it's just a short dash across the sand to the chopper.

"Get out of there, chump," roars Gung-Ho at the pilot. "We just canceled your flight plan."

Before the pilot can react, Dusty grabs him and holds him while Gung-Ho puts out his lights with one chop.

"This hasn't been a good trip for pilots," says Lady Jaye.

"It goes like that sometimes," Duke replies, and the trace of a grin begins across his serious face.

....
Turn to page 11.

"Let's return to the palace—we'll be less noticeable there," you decide.

The ride back seems so much longer than the ride there. But you make it eventually.

The palace is deserted. Are COBRA Commander and his crew already on their way to Mt. Terrapin with the poltron? You go to the spot where Lady Jaye hid her communicator. She kneels and slips back the loose brick that's covering the hiding place—and the communicator isn't there!

"Here it is!" you yell. The communicator had fallen behind the wall in some sandy soil. But it functions fine. You make contact!

You can hear Duke's voice on the other end. He assures you that a flotilla of subs will make sure the poltron never reaches Mt. Terrapin. You assure him that you've got The One in custody. And then you hear the words you've been waiting for.

"Hey, guys, come on home—this mission is a wrap!"

THE END

The footsteps stop right in front of your face. "What an appropriate position. We've brought G.I. Joe to his knees," a voice sneers.

Your blindfold is snatched off. You jump to your feet and are face-to-hood with COBRA Commander. Flanking him are the beautiful COBRA operative known as the Baroness, who flashes you an evil smile; Storm Shadow, COBRA Commander's Ninja bodyguard; and Destro, the weapons supplier, faceless behind his silver mask. Behind them hangs a portrait of The One.

"Take him away," COBRA Commander snaps at two guards.

The guards lead you through a maze of hallways, all decorated with drawings, photos, and statues of The One. Obviously, this is his headquarters.

You are searched and then slammed into a small cell. You feel as if the walls are closing in.

You've got to get a hold of yourself. You do have options: There's the hidden arsenal of weapons in your shoe. Would your fold-up file work on these bars? Or what about your pick? You practiced on hundreds of locks in training.

But if you bust out, which way do you go back through the maze? Are there sensors? There must be heavy security here. Would you be walking right into a trap?

Quick—before they come back—you must decide.

....

Do you try to break out? Turn to page 4.
Or do you cool it and sit tight? Turn to page 32.

You're sure sitting tight is the right thing. But you hate waiting. Patience is not one of your strong points. You try to keep your mind active. In your head, you take apart, clean, and reassemble all the Joe weapons. You practice French verbs.

But you lose track of time. When your meals come, you don't know if they're lunch or dinner.

You drift. You dream a big dog is being shoved through the bars at you. You jolt awake.

It's no dog. It's Quick Kick, bound with ropes.

"Quick Kick, I can't believe they caught you! I mean, this is my first mission, but you...!"

"Don't feel bad. It happens to the best of us sometimes," says Quick Kick. "And I'm here to spring you."

"You mean...?" you begin, astonished.

"That's right. I let myself be taken. After all, we don't like to see our own kind rotting away in cells, right?"

"Right," you grin, "but what's our next step?"

"It's not going to be easy," he says.

Turn to page 82.

You watch in horror while the Baroness points an accusing finger at Lady Jaye, and Lady Jaye points an accusing finger at the Baroness.

Finally, you see Lady Jaye being handcuffed. It's probably useless, but you've got to try to save her!

You jump into a van, turn on the ignition, and floor it. COBRA Commander and Destro look on with terror as you come barreling down the dock. Everybody scatters as you pull up, which lets you make a wide turn, skid to a stop, snatch up Lady Jaye, and tear off again, burning rubber.

It's a spectacular exit—but it's a little obvious. COBRA troops spring up from every side. They fire at your tires as you keep your pedal to the metal and speed away. Well, not quite away. The last thing you see is a brick wall.

Too bad you didn't see it just a few seconds before you came to a crashing...

END

Using a secret escape route that is known only to The One, you, Lady Jaye, Quick Kick, and The One himself sneak out of the palace. You borrow a jeep and drive over nearly impossible roads as The One directs you to the poltron processing plant.

"They probably won't let us in," says The One. "They're all COBRA men guarding the place now."

"No problem," says Quick Kick.

With very little effort, you and your teammates overpower the guards. Inside, the plant is pretty well deserted, except for some sounds of activity coming from the shipping docks.

Sneaking through the plant quietly, you come across crate after crate of poltron gas marked TERRAPIN.

"Terrapin!" Lady Jaye gasps. "Now I know what COBRA is up to! These are headed for the U.S. base on Mt. Terrapin."

"That's a missile base, isn't it?" you ask. But you don't really want to hear the answer. Is COBRA going after U.S. missiles now?

Lady Jaye reads your thoughts. "COBRA would never risk an attack on that base with the usual weapons. It's too heavily guarded. But with the poltron gas, all they have to do..." Her voice trails off.

"...is fly nearby and let loose with the stuff," you finish. "The army will turn over everything voluntarily!"

....

Turn to page 15.

Slipping away isn't hard. It's slipping into the radio room and getting your message out to the Joe Team that's more difficult. But you do it!

You're in the process of sending your message when all of a sudden the door crashes open. Two armed COBRAS are standing with their weapons pointed right at you. Behind them are two more guards, with the Baroness—the *real* Baroness—and Quick Kick in tow.

They grab you and throw you into the back of a van. Quick Kick is thrown in next to you. You don't speak. What is there to say?

You drive through streets of half-finished buildings. At last, you arrive at the pier, where a sleek, ocean-going ship is docked. Crate after crate of poltron gas is being loaded onto the ship. The crates are marked TERRAPIN.

Is there anything *you can do? Turn to page 55.*

Disregarding the warning, you stay on course. The winds rage against the plane. You struggle to hold on to the controls as the craft is battered and bounced like a Ping-Pong ball. You drop dangerously close to the mountains below, and then a strong gust lifts you spinning to a higher but even windier altitude.

The cockpit door opens behind you. "Ride 'em, cowboy!" Gung-Ho yells in encouragement. "If you can *think* it, you can *do* it. That's what my momma always said!"

You have a hard time imagining that this hulk ever had a mother. But you take his advice. You think only good thoughts. You *think* the plane down. You grab on to the bouncing, vibrating controls and *think* of a small runway in a mountain pass above the desert near the Kamali-Mombania border.

And sure enough, you find one. The wind makes one last effort to tear the plane apart, but you burst through it...

...and land with a back-wrenching *thud,* bouncing across the narrow runway and stopping just where the concrete gives way to rocky soil.

"No offense, good buddy," Gung-Ho says, "but next time, I think I'll take the train!"

"Let's check out our location," Duke says.

But Dusty has already thrown open the door. "Uh-oh!" he cries. "Hey, Duke—we're not alone!"

Turn to page 46.

The guard's rifle flies into the air. You make a desperate leap for it and bring it down. You drive the rifle butt deep into the guard's stomach.

Quick Kick's feet find their target again, and the second guard falls to the floor. Destro raises a small pistol and aims it at Quick Kick, but you raise the rifle and blast the pistol from his hand.

You turn the rifle toward the Baroness, who raises her hands in surrender. "Where's COBRA Commander?" you yell, untying Quick Kick's ropes.

Quick Kick only shrugs. COBRA Commander has somehow vanished into thin air.

"Let's not worry about him—let's just get outta here!" you scream, keeping the rifle trained on Destro and the Baroness.

Quick Kick shatters a window with his boot. "Geronimo!" he yells, leaping out. You look to see if any more COBRA guards are on the way. Seeing none, you follow him out the window.

A few moments later, the two of you are safely on your way back to HQ. "Geronimo?" you say.

"That's an ancient Oriental expression," he says with a grin.

"We've got the info we need. COBRA *is* behind The One. But we didn't get COBRA Commander," you say, disappointed.

"Here's another old Oriental expression," Quick Kick replies. "Tomorrow is another day...."

THE END

Just then you hear a faint sound coming from a distance behind you. No, it can't be. But it is!

It's the backup team! It wasn't a bluff. They did get your message!

And then on the horizon, you see hovercraft emerging from the water and tanks approaching on land!

COBRA Commander and company are stunned. Obviously, they didn't develop a Plan B. As the Joe Team closes in and the COBRAS gear up for battle, there's utter confusion. You are able to free yourself from your guards.

It's clear that COBRA Commander, the Baroness, and Destro have one thing on their minds—saving their own hides. You see them disappearing into a waiting submarine. You want to go after them, but there's no time. They're gone.

You've lost the big ones, but you may still come out of this alive! You pull the turtleneck of your sweater over your nose to fashion a makeshift gas mask. Then you rip open one of the crates of poltron gas and begin to release a canister of the stuff in the direction of several COBRA troopers. The stuff is amazing! One by one the COBRAS throw down their arms and give up. The sound of their whimpering soon replaces the sound of bullets.

· ·

Turn to page 89.

You've got to stick close to Lady Jaye. You don't know how the two of you are going to stop that shipment of poltron from leaving Kamali, but somehow you've got to.

You get into a van along with some other guards and pretend to be sleepy while the others chatter away.

The van bumps over impossible roads, screeching around hairpin turns. You are going down a hill rapidly, toward Kamali City, which is under construction.

You go around the outskirts, where several enormous buildings are being built. You finally reach a series of piers that look as if they were finished yesterday. From several of them, there are crates upon crates being loaded onto sleek, ocean-going ships.

Your blood runs cold. Getting out of the van, you see Lady Jaye and COBRA Commander. Destro is there too.

Watching from a distance, you try to figure out your next move.

But before long, it's decided for you.

A car comes racing onto the pier, and from it step the guard whom Quick Kick had knocked out earlier and the Baroness—the *real* Baroness!

Turn to page 33.

You check out the entire exterior of the house, walking around it in a big circle. You find nothing but broken windows and rotting shingles.

"Have we chased the wild goose this time?" you ask Quick Kick.

"I don't know. Let's get to the heart of the matter."

Quick Kick doesn't pussyfoot around. He takes a short running start and, with a single thrust of his right leg, smashes in a large window.

When the dust clears, you climb through. It's very dim inside, but slowly you focus on a large, empty living room. Empty, that is, except for enough cobwebs and dust to fill three Saturday-afternoon horror films.

Beside you, Quick Kick gasps, "Aaaaargh!"

You wheel to see what's wrong, but you have enough trouble of your own. Hands grab you from behind, bind, blindfold, and gag you. You're dragged down a hall and pushed into an elevator that drops like your hopes.

Turn to page 70.

41

"Do you know how you were programmed by COBRA?" Duke asks.

You shake your head. Something about electricity, or was it an injection? You're not sure.

"Let me look at him," says Lady Jaye. She carefully inspects your arms and pulls your hair back from your forehead. She murmurs something to Duke.

You don't remember what was done to you to bring your mind back from COBRA's grasp. But once you're back in your right mind, you're sure glad they did it. And thanks to the deprogramming, you are able to help by giving them some inside information about the security system at the palace.

As the G.I. Joe Team gets ready to storm the palace, your head is still full of questions. What is the secret of The One's power? Why is COBRA involved here? You don't know. But you're glad you've been able to play some part in this adventure, although not in quite the way you had planned.

THE END

"Either it's dinnertime or bedtime—forever," says the guard with the machine gun. He pokes you with the UZI's deadly barrel. "And feed your buddy, too."

You eat a spoonful of the disgusting mess. It's some kind of stew with noodles. It looks like something from your old school cafeteria. But somehow, you've got to keep the garbage down.

However, that turns out not to be such a hot idea.

Within moments your eyes blur and your stomach is churning. Your tongue is thick. Your head feels like a gong.

"Mxputtle," a guard says. You try to listen more carefully. "Rumpulstikky." Nothing is making sense.

Then it dawns on you. Poison! You try to tell Quick Kick, but you can't get the words out.

It doesn't matter. He's doubled up in a tight ball and his eyes are rolled back in his head.

The room is beginning to spin so fast that you can't keep up with it. And it's growing dimmer. Are your lights going out?

Is this the end?

Turn to page 26.

It seems like only moments, and a Joe Team is standing before you—led by a grinning Roadblock.

"Let's get on with this," he says, rubbing his hands together. "Can't wait to sink my teeth into this one—COBRA's even tastier than filet mignon!" Same old Roadblock—always thinking about gourmet food.

Back at The One's mansion, all is quiet and still. It looks like a haunted house. All it needs is a few bats flying around.

"I'll lead, along with Dog Ear," says Roadblock as the front door swings open. He claps you on the shoulder. "Point the way."

Down, down, down you go again. But this time with your eyes wide open. However, real estate is all there is to see. There's not a soul in sight.

"Stuck on himself, huh?" Roadblock says in the quiet. You jump and look where he's pointing. Ah, the huge picture of The One. Otherwise, nothing.

"I think we're wasting our time," says Roadblock. "I think they've blown."

"Wait!" says Quick Kick. You wheel toward him. He has his finger against his lips.

"Listen," he says. "Do you hear that ticking?"

....
Turn to page 49.

44

"Awright!" says Dusty. "That's more like it!"

After burying the deceased pilot, you, Duke, Dusty, Gung-Ho, and Lady Jaye gather as many supplies as you can carry and head out.

The days are blazing hot. The nights are icy cold. As the days pass, both supplies and enthusiasm are dwindling—except for Dusty's, of course. Somehow this isn't nearly as much fun as you thought it was going to be.

Finally you clear the mountains. You all stand at the top and there below you is—more sand. And more sand. It stretches on forever.

"Dawgone," says Gung-Ho. "Us swamp boys could get real dry in a climate like this."

But what is that on the horizon? Are you imagining it? No, it looks an awful lot like an oasis. Palm trees, water hole—and is that a camel?

"Look!" you point.

Lady Jaye follows your finger. "Gosh, I thought I was seeing a mirage like in the old desert movies. But if you see it, too, it must be real."

"Move it, guys," says Gung-Ho. "This old alligator could use a good wallow."

· ·

Turn to page 58.

"Grab your weapons!" Duke commands.

"No need," Dusty calls from outside the plane. "It's just a bunch of desert nomads, only about ten of 'em, and they look pretty harmless."

You, Duke, Gung-Ho, and Lady Jaye, rifles in hand, leap out of the plane. The small band of nomads approaches the landing strip. The men wear heavy robes and hoods despite the heat. They travel on foot. A scraggly donkey loaded down with supplies follows.

The leader walks up to you, bows, and speaks in a language you've never heard. Duke replies immediately. His days at the Army Special Language School were not wasted! After a brief conversation, he turns to you and the other team members.

"They saw our plane go down and came to help us," Duke says. "They'll lead us part of the way to Kamali City."

You trail the small band of nomads, following a twisting path through the rocky cliffs. The sky grows dark. It appears there may be a storm. Suddenly, the nomads come to a stop. They turn to face you. They tear off their hoods, reach under their robes, and pull out machine guns. Under their robes, you see their all-too-familiar uniforms!

"COBRA!" you scream.

Turn to page 76.

46

You're a tough pilot, but the storm looks even tougher. So you decide to bring the plane down in the desert now! Though this could be tough, too. The desert just inside Mombania, across the mountains from Kamali, may be Dusty's idea of a little bit of heaven, but not yours.

Bump...Bump...Kaplow! Deserts aren't as flat as they look on maps. But you've landed safely. Everyone is shaken up, although happy to be on solid ground.

"Let's just sit tight in here until these winds die down," says Duke. "Walking out there now would be like walking into a wall of sandpaper."

"Aw, come on, let's—" Dusty pleads.

"Forget it, Dusty. You'll just have to wait until morning."

Dusty is still sleeping when Gung-Ho sticks his head out the door the next day. "Holy crawdad," he says. "Will you look at that!"

The plane is buried halfway up in sand.

Dusty scratches his head. "Well, we could start digging—"

"I'm no sandhog," says Lady Jaye. "Even if we dug for a week, we'd still be here. And mighty dry."

"You're right," says Duke. "We can't get this bird up again. We'll have to take our chances," he says, pointing into the vast wasteland, "out there."

....
Turn to page 45.

Do you? All of a sudden, in the stillness, you can hear nothing else but.

"It's a time bomb about to go!" shouts Road-block.

Tick-tick. Tick-tick.

You can hear the last seconds of your life ticking off.

"Run!" Roadblock pushes you. "COBRA lured us back in and now they're going to blow us to smithereens!"

"Welcome to the end!" a creepy voice says suddenly from nowhere. "Don't bother to look for me. This is just a recorded message." It's COBRA_Commander! "Now there's a lesson to be learned here. It's not nice to trespass where you aren't invited. You might remember that next time. If you believe in a next time."

His hideous laugh sends chills down your spine.

"Don't bother to run. All the doors have been resealed upon your entry. And now for the countdown.

"Five ... four ... three ... two ... one ..." You know the rest....

THE END

"Dog Ear, it's me, Quick Kick. Don't you know me?" asks the enemy soldier.

"Death to G.I. Joe," you say automatically. You can't figure out where that phrase came from. You're not even sure you know what it means.

Quick Kick approaches you.

"I warn you. Stand back," you hear yourself saying.

"Dog Ear," he says again. You wonder if that's a kind of curse.

You aim your submachine gun at the man, but he's too fast for you, knocking it from your grasp with his foot.

This strange-looking guy, who seems to know you—now he's taken your gun away.

Something in a dim corner of your mind flashes a familiar picture. Could you have met him before? And fought him?

Two other strangers are on you suddenly and begin dragging you down the corridor. Something is telling you to go with them. You wonder if they have hypnotized you!

You have to decide whether to go with your strange instinct—or with your COBRA duty.

....

If you decide to call out for help from COBRA, turn to page 65.

If you decide to let yourself be taken captive, turn to page 53.

50

"Now where?" you ask Bulldog.

"Keep your yap shut and keep walking toward that door." He pushes you with the gun toward Vanderbilt Avenue. "I've got a car waiting."

He shoves you into the backseat of a black Mercedes, squeezes in after you, and slams the door. You jump! Bad sign, letting him see your nerves. You've got to cool it.

The driver, an East Asian, turns and hands you a blindfold.

"No thanks, I don't need a handkerchief."

Cool, but the guy definitely doesn't think it's funny. He leans back and grabs you by an ear and jerks you forward. You bite your lip at the pain.

"There, smart guy." He's tied the bandanna very tight.

You must remember the sounds and try to keep track of the distance as you are riding, but it's hard. Especially with *no* sounds. It's like a tomb in the Mercedes.

"Don't let me interrupt your conversation," you say.

"Zip it, mister," Bulldog grunts.

So you "zip it" like baggage. That's how they're treating you. That's how you should act. But they should remember that baggage can hold surprises.

·····································

Turn to page 84.

You play it cool and pretend to ignore Bulldog. You stroll casually over to a magazine shop and thumb through a martial-arts magazine.

Suddenly you see Bulldog's square body lunge into the doorway. You focus on a picture in your magazine and before you can say "Bruce Lee," Bulldog has pressed a gun barrel into your back.

"One false move and you're dead, Joe," he whispers.

"I think you have the wrong guy," you whisper back. "My name's not Joe."

His voice isn't friendly. "You know what I mean, tough guy. Now move it!"

You take a split-second look out the shop door. Quick Kick is nowhere in sight. You're on your own.

With the gun barrel, Bulldog pushes you toward the waiting room. If he shoots there, civilians will be in danger.

Now's the time, Dog Ear. Quickly.

....

Do you clobber him with the tricks you learned from Bruce Lee and Quick Kick and run? Turn to page 79.

Or do you follow along and see where he leads you? Turn to page 51.

52

You relax and let yourself be carried out of the palace without a fight. It's strange. Some part of you feels a great sense of relief.

Quickly your captors pull you away from the palace grounds.

"Well, Dog Ear, you had us worried for a while," says the man who called himself Quick Kick.

"Uh, fellows," you answer, "who's this Dog Ear?"

They look at one another.

"We've got ourselves a bigger problem than we thought," says Gung-Ho.

Back at the Joe Team camp, a woman they call Lady Jaye gives you a big hug. "Oh, Dog Ear," she says. "This is carrying role-playing too far. But you aren't playing, are you?"

Duke, the tall blond man, questions you about COBRA.

"I think COBRA took over from The One, but I'm not too sure about anything," you say. "I feel really confused and I have a terrible headache."

"I'm afraid this is going to hurt even more," says Duke, "but we're going to have to deprogram you. It's your only hope—and ours."

....

Turn to page 42.

Deciding to sneak into the meeting is one thing. Getting in is another. But you get a lucky break. You spot the Baroness in the hall with only a single guard.

You zip into action. Quick Kick puts the guard away while you and Lady Jaye overpower the Baroness. Dragging her quickly into a tiny supply room you've discovered, Lady Jaye swiftly goes about exchanging identities with the evil COBRA operative.

You knew Lady Jaye was good at disguise. But you didn't know she was *that* good. The set of her jaw, her voice, her posture—she looks so much like the Baroness, you begin to doubt your own eyes.

Leaving Quick Kick in charge of the two unconscious enemies, you—in the guard's uniform—and Lady Jaye as the Baroness hurry down the hall toward the meeting room.

Will COBRA Commander be fooled? Turn to page 78 and find out!

You and Quick Kick are shoved off the van, and then onto one of the piers. At the end of it you can see COBRA Commander, Destro, and Lady Jaye.

Even if you could think of something clever to do, there's no time to do it. COBRA Commander has spotted you—and the real Baroness. He looks strangely at Lady Jaye next to him, then orders her placed under arrest.

You and Quick Kick are brought side by side with the disguised Lady Jaye.

"It looks like you've outfoxed yourselves," says COBRA Commander to the three of you. "Now, let's see, would you like to accompany the shipment of poltron to the other side of the globe and be dropped along with it over your own military base? Or would you rather be fed to the sharks?" He's a real witty guy.

You've got no cards to play. So you bluff.

"I've radioed our backup, and they're on their way right now to crush you," you blurt out. "You don't have a chance."

"Don't make me laugh," says COBRA Commander.

Turn to page 38.

The G.I. Joe Team does not take orders from two-bit soldiers in movie costumes. At the same time, all five of you reach for your guns and let the nearest soldiers have it.

You haven't any idea what you're planning to do next. But your options are pretty limited.

There are more soldiers than you thought, and the shooting has brought still others out of the fort—a low whitewashed building that doesn't look as if it could even keep a camel out.

All of you run in different directions. Out of the corner of your eye, you see Duke, then Gung-Ho, then Lady Jaye being taken prisoner. You have no doubt that they'll put up a good fight.

Dusty is nowhere to be seen. For some reason, the soldiers have overlooked you. Maybe it's just not your turn.

Hiding behind a large palm, you watch as the soldiers parade your three teammates off to the fort.

But where is Dusty? He must have escaped into the desert—his natural habitat. You decide to try to join him.

Go on to page 57.

Once out of view of the fort, you feel a bit safer. But you must think clearly, develop a plan. The desert is not forgiving. One slip-up, and bye-bye, Dog Ear.

You spot a huge sand drift that you can use as a landmark. You'll keep it on your left as you walk. Then you won't get lost, right? Wrong. You're soon walking in circles. You're hopelessly lost.

The day is blistering hot. You didn't have a chance to refill your canteen at the oasis. You could go back, except now you can't find the oasis.

You grow faint with thirst and exhaustion. But you've got to get a grip on yourself. You try a mental game you were taught in training. You close your eyes and visualize your goal.

You imagine Dusty, his goggles perched on top of his head. And when you open your eyes, there he is! You wave at him in the distance.

"Dusty, Dusty." He's too far. He can't hear you.

You run toward him, faster and faster and...

Thunk. You're facedown in the sand. You look up and he's gone. Then you realize it was only a mirage. You don't have the strength to go on.

Sorry, Dog Ear. Looks like you hit a dry hole this time!

THE END

This is no mirage. It's a real oasis. The tiny town looks just like a set from a French Foreign Legion movie.

Lady Jaye approaches the owner of a shop and speaks to him in his own language. The shopkeeper is wary of the strikingly beautiful woman, sunburnt and wearing sand-encrusted clothes. After all, this is a land where women still hide behind their veils.

"Poor guy," Lady Jaye says, returning with food. "He's had a bad week. The forces of The One have seized this area and claimed it for Kamali. They're in a fort just down there." She points down the street from the market where you stand.

As if on cue, from that direction storm three dozen soldiers with dark flashing eyes, white desert robes, and very nasty-looking swords.

Whoosh! Slash! Swish! The sound of the swords whirling around your heads is not amusing.

A dashing fellow rides up to you on a dazzlingly white Arabian horse. "You will not reach for your guns," he says. "You will reach for the sky."

Do you decide to ignore him and fight it out? Turn to page 56.

If you decide you're hopelessly outnumbered and had better surrender, turn to page 27.

58

Hanging around this cell is your idea of nothing to do, but finding out what's going on here is your mission.

"Patience is a virtue," whispers Quick Kick. "My ancestors teach that wisdom comes through being still, like a pond."

You know that there is truth in his Oriental teachings. You will try. But you feel antsy, more like a river full of white-water rapids than a still pond.

After a few hours, you hear footsteps.

"See," Quick Kick whispers. "The action comes to us."

And it does. Two guards arrive. One is carrying a tray with your dinner. The other is carrying a nice neat UZI.

"Dinnertime," says the guard with the tray.

"Now!" says the guard with the machine gun.

"I don't think we're hungry," you respond.

"Why don't you let your buddy here speak for himself?" the guard says.

"We believe in saving our breath—especially with COBRAS," you reply.

Quick Kick frowns. You realize that your smart mouth hasn't learned a thing about patience. But it's too late now!

Turn to page 43.

"Time's a-wasting," you tell Quick Kick. "I'm not hanging around this dump until dinnertime."

Using his pick, Quick Kick quietly opens the door and you creep out into a corridor. There's no one around. Could this be a trap?

After what seems like miles, you come to a door to the outside. Suddenly you hear loud voices.

"I think Building A should go up two more stories."

"Not if we put the prisons underground."

Quick Kick motions to you, and you both run out the door. You stumble, and when you look up, you can't find Quick Kick. You twist to the right and, holding your breath, roll under some low bushes.

You lie there struggling for a plan. You're dead tired. The men have entered the building you just escaped from, so you can't go back in. You're on your own, in enemy territory.

Forward, then. With a quick check to make sure no one's in sight, you leave the compound behind and make your way through dense foliage. Finally, you just can't make it any farther. You lie down under a date palm and rest.

Turn to page 75.

Then one day, still feeling very dizzy and strange, you find yourself standing before COBRA Commander.

"Greetings, Dog Ear," he says.

"Who is Dog Ear?" you answer. "I am Corporal Sanza reporting for duty. Hail to COBRA."

"Who is The One?" COBRA Commander asks.

"The One is he who rules this country—he thinks. But you rule him, Great COBRA."

"Take your position, Corporal Sanza," he says, smiling. "I'm sure we can count on you."

Of course he can. How could he doubt you?

As the days pass, you follow your COBRA instructions without question, hoping for a chance to prove yourself.

One day you hear gunfire in the distance. This is your chance to prove your loyalty to COBRA. The gunshots grow closer. You begin to tingle with excitement. You're going to get to show your stuff!

Enemy foot soldiers attack The One's palace where you stand guard. Others are flying in on rocketpacks. Suddenly you're face-to-face with one of the intruders. As you raise your arm to clobber him, you look into his eyes. He reminds you of someone. Perhaps from a dream...

....

Turn to page 50.

You tense your muscles, ready to run. You want to get rid of this guy—now! But you remember your training. Hold it—for the right moment.

There it is! A large family wheels a dolly loaded with suitcases between you and Bulldog.

You slip through the crowd and spot a perfect hiding place. You jump over and behind the counter of a startled pizza cook.

"Shhhhh!" You put one finger to your lips.

He begins whistling and keeps twirling pizza. He's not going to give you away.

You hear steps coming toward you. Then they stop right in front of the stand. Still the pizza man whistles. Then the same steps walk quickly away in the direction of the waiting room.

"Let's hear it for the boy..." The pizza man breaks into song, as if someone hid behind his counter every day.

Is this a good time to leave your cover?

···
If you want to make a dash for it now, turn to page 13.

If you think you should stay hidden a little longer to be sure, turn to page 85.

63

Your heart pounds as you race down the long tiled corridor that leads to the subway. You dodge commuters who never look up as they, too, hurry toward their destinations.

At the last minute, instead of going down the steps to the subway, you execute a quick right turn, then a left, and duck into a telephone booth.

Whew! You lean over and try to catch your breath.

Looking up from wiping your face with your handkerchief, you are staring dead into the business end of a revolver. The overhead lights glint off its silencer. Behind it stands Bulldog, with a ghastly grin on his face.

"There's no way out, you know," he says. "I'd give you a quarter to call for help, but I don't have any change."

No, Dog Ear, a G.I. Joe who overestimates his skills never gets another chance. He doesn't even get to call headquarters to say good-bye. But you'll have to say good-bye, Dog Ear—because this is...

THE END

"Help!" you cry. "I'm being kidnapped!"

A group of four COBRAS fighting nearby take one look and race to your rescue. They batter the G.I. Joe unit with the butts of their rifles.

You join in, too. You've got to show COBRA Commander where you stand.

Right in the middle, that's where.

POW! SOCK! SMASH! CRUNCH!

Wow! You're crunching people right and left. And another right. And another left.

Soon the Joe Team is so weak they can barely turn tail and run. But they do. Out of the palace. And out of the country. COBRA has won! Your heart is pounding with joy!

Enjoy your moment of victory while you can. You won't be celebrating in a month or two when the brainwashing wears off. Then you will have to face the awful truth. Quick, close the book before the word *traitor* pounds too loudly in your ears!

THE END

You feel good about your decision to go to Africa with Lady Jaye, Duke, Gung-Ho, and Dusty. After all, you need to learn a few things about this mission, and you'll take advantage of the time on the plane with the others to iron out the questions.

In half an hour, a jeep drops you at a remote landing strip in New Jersey. A prop jet is waiting. But it's so small! Dusty catches your disappointed look.

"Buck up, partner," he says. "You ain't seen nothing."

In another hour you're piling into a gigantic camouflaged jet on an even more remote airstrip—somewhere.

"You might as well try to get some shut-eye," Lady Jaye says when you're all buckled in. "It'll be eight hours before we land on the border between The One's kingdom, Kamali, and Mombania, the country to the west. Then you'll need to be in A-One shape. We have to work fast scoping out the scene for the other members of the Team who'll join us later."

You're sleeping like a baby, dreaming of Kamali, when suddenly you're jolted awake. Your stomach is above your head as you plummet through the air like a stone.

The plane is losing altitude quickly. If you don't hurry, you're going to lose more than that!

Go on to page 67.

"Go!" Gung-Ho urges you. "You're the one who's a pilot!"

Your teammates' lives are in your hands. You tear open the door to the cockpit and there is the pilot, draped across the controls, *dead*!

His eyes are glassy. His face is blue. A heart attack? Better that than foul play. Because if it's poison or strangling, if there's a traitor...you put the possibilities out of your mind. You don't have time to *think*.

You grab the controls. The instrument panel is one you've never seen before. But you act instinctively, pulling the plane out of its nose dive, fighting its destructive downward momentum. Up, up, up, and you've almost got it when the radio crackles.

"Hurricane force winds ahead. Reroute! Reroute!"

You have to decide. You can ignore the warnings and try to land where you're scheduled to, in the mountains of Kamali. Or you can try an emergency landing now, in the Mombanian desert. That could be tricky.

....

If you want to ride out the storm and land in the mountains of Kamali, turn to page 36.

Or if you want to avoid the storm and take your chances in the Mombanian desert, turn to page 48.

67

The next morning, your strength is back and you're ready for action. You, Lady Jaye, and Quick Kick head for The One's palace. You go over your cover story once again: You've escaped from a prison in Mombania, made your way across the country, and have vowed revenge by joining up with The One. It sounds believable—to you, anyway.

And your background? Soldiers of fortune, each of you. The three of you are now a team, having weathered several campaigns together. One for all and all for one.

The guards at The One's palace gate look you over carefully before using their radios to call somebody on the inside to come get you. You can tell they don't get many visitors here, because they seem ill at ease.

You are admitted to the palace and taken through hall after hall. There are pictures and statues of The One everywhere. Some people come to Africa on safari, but this guy's come on an ego trip!

You see no COBRA uniforms; the guards look as if they're wearing army surplus. You have to figure out what's going on. You are taken to a room where a man sits behind a desk. "These three want to become palace guards," your guide says to the man.

....
Go on to page 69.

Out of the corner of your eye, you catch a glimpse of Storm Shadow, COBRA Commander's Ninja bodyguard. You know his appearance well from photos. There's no doubt that COBRA is in thick with The One—but how thick?

You have no problem doing your job as palace guards. And eventually, you become bolder about listening in at keyholes and lingering in corners. One day you overhear a voice:

"Well, if COBRA Commander says waste him, we waste him. The One is such a fool! He thinks COBRA Commander would do all this for him without wanting something for himself."

Another voice says, "We've reprogrammed almost all The One's men. They think COBRA now. Just a few days to go and we'll get rid of that clown!"

Your eyes open wide. You track down Lady Jaye and Quick Kick and tell them what you've heard. You have a decision to make.

Should you warn The One that COBRA plans to assassinate him? If you do, he might give you enough information and ammunition to fight COBRA.

Or do you think it's too risky to warn him? Maybe you should just stick by him and protect him.

If you want to warn The One, turn to page 25.
If you decide not to, turn to page 77.

Your blindfold is ripped off. The light is overpowering. Then you see a larger-than-life portrait of The One.

"So," a voice sneers behind you, "G.I. Joe has arrived. You keep popping up everywhere, like cockroaches." You wheel around. It's COBRA Commander.

"I don't think we've seen this one before." He's speaking to a pretty woman wearing glasses whom you recognize as the Baroness. On her right is a man in a silver mask who can only be Destro, the arms supplier.

"It's nice of you to drop in," COBRA Commander says, turning back to you. "We're always glad to have company."

His high-pitched laugh is bone-chilling. Then he motions to the guards to tie Quick Kick's hands. Obviously he knows Quick Kick's talents.

Turn to page 6.

"Come on, we can't waste any time," you say. "Let's radio from here!"

The One leads you around to the radio control room. You haven't been spotted by COBRA, and you hope to keep it that way. Luckily, the control room is deserted.

Quick Kick stands watch at the door while the rest of you enter the small room.

"Know how to use this stuff?" Lady Jaye asks The One. He shrugs. "Never mind," she says and starts fiddling with the knobs. "Now let's hope I can get a message through to G.I. Joe! The fate of the entire world may be at stake!"

Suddenly you hear a scuffle outside. You investigate and see Quick Kick being confronted by four COBRA soldiers. You know he's fighting off his impulse to strike out at them—and so are you. But you have to act as if there's nothing unusual about your being in the radio room.

"Afternoon, soldiers," you say, poking your head out the door. "Just listening to the Super Bowl on the short wave. How about those Dolphins?"

"Kid thinks he's smart," says one of the COBRAS. "Smart is good sometimes, and sometimes it is not so good."

This time, it's not so good. The COBRAS break in before Lady Jaye can make radio contact, and they don't buy your cover. They don't buy your phony uniforms. They don't buy your sense of humor. But you, Quick Kick, Lady Jaye, and The One buy the farm. Bye-bye.

THE END

71

"Let's do it!" you say, pulling your laser knife from the heel of your shoe.

"Good show!" Quick Kick says, and stares with interest as the knife expands until it's a good six inches long.

You cut through his ropes and then back out of his way. Even a friend doesn't want to be in Quick Kick's range when he's stretching those death-dealing hands and feet!

Next you turn to try the laser knife on the cell bars.

"Out of my way," Quick Kick interrupts you and then...

KAZAM! Quick Kick takes the quick and dirty way out. He winds up and thrusts out his left foot. *KAPLOW!* Where the bars were is now air.

But the noise has stirred up more than just some metal bars.

Footsteps are running toward you. They're almost here. Which way should you run?

To the right? Turn to page 83.
To the left? Turn to page 23.

72

But there is another surprise in store for you and the other members of the G.I. Joe Team. As you reach the top of the ridge, your eyes struggle to adjust to the bright sunlight that casts a blinding glare.

Shielding your burning eyes with both hands, you see directly in front of you ... *an entire battalion of COBRA soldiers!*

A cry of alarm goes up in the COBRA camp. You've been spotted! Grenade throwers are turned toward you. Automatic rifle fire shatters the desert silence.

"There must be at least a hundred of them!" you cry.

"Retreat!" Duke yells, dropping to the sand.

"We can take 'em!" Gung-Ho yells over the gunfire. He raises his M-16 and fires back. "There ain't that many of 'em! We've had bigger odds before! Let's go get 'em and get to Kamali City!"

"No!" Duke protests. "Our first job is to radio the info we've gotten back to HQ! We've got to head back to the plane!"

You must quickly decide what to do.

....

Retreat to the plane and radio headquarters? Turn to page 7.

Follow Gung-Ho's lead and fight the COBRAS? Turn to page 86.

In seconds, you're dreaming. You're back in the van. Quick Kick is being tossed in alongside you. He's broken loose from his ropes. He's shaking you and shaking you. Why won't he stop?

You reach out to stop him and jolt awake. That's a real hand you touched! You open your eyes. It's the hand of Gung-Ho.

"Hi there, little buddy!" Gung-Ho gives you a slap on the back that almost knocks the wind out of you. "We've been waiting for you for ages! Glad you could make it."

"Me too," you answer faintly.

"Looks to me like you could use some grub. Come on, and I'll put some Cajun swamp stew in you."

Then you see Quick Kick, Duke, Dusty, and Lady Jaye. Somehow Quick Kick managed to reconnoiter with the G.I. Joe Team! And somehow you're all together.

You all sit down over some bowls of Gung-Ho's stew and Duke reviews the mission assignments.

Gung-Ho, Dusty, and Duke are going into the neighboring country of Mombania to check on COBRA activities there. You, Lady Jaye, and Quick Kick are on your way to infiltrate The One's palace.

....

Turn to page 68.

75

"We seem to have fallen into a trap," Lady Jaye says, as you all stare at the COBRAS' machine guns. "They must be working with The One."

"Not necessarily," Duke says. "They may be here for the same reason we are—to get information. Let me try to talk to them."

But the COBRAS aim their machine guns and prepare to fire. There isn't going to be any conversation.

Suddenly, a bolt of lightning flashes across the sky. The ground rumbles from the roar of thunder. Another lightning flash, blinding in intensity, lights up the scene like a floodlight.

This distraction is all you need. All five of you leap at the COBRAS, catching them off guard. "This'll teach you to try and trick *this* ragin' Cajun!" Gung-Ho yells, battering a startled COBRA with his own machine gun.

One of the COBRAS panics and begins firing his weapon, taking down two of his own men. You've got to grab the weapon from him before he hits one of your team members. You toss an attacking COBRA off your back, give him a hard kick with your boot to keep him down, and lunge forward with all your strength.

You've got to grab the roaring machine gun. . . . You've *got* to!

Turn to page 14.

In the next few days you make it a point to know where The One is at all times. Unfortunately, you can't always get to where he is. There are a number of places along the twisting palace corridors where only the elite personal guards are allowed.

One day, Storm Shadow enters The One's private chambers while you and Lady Jaye are reporting to him. Storm Shadow approaches The One. Your hand tenses around your weapon. Your eyes never leave his. Is this the moment he will strike? No. He bows, turns away, and leaves. You relax, confident that you have protected The One.

Then you smell it. A strange sweet, over-powering smell. It comes from a pellet no bigger than a button that someone has dropped right by The One's feet.

Do we have to spell it out for you? The pellet has a poison gas so powerful that you can do nothing but sigh as you take your last breath. Storm Shadow has put the first part of COBRA's plan into effect. Be grateful you won't be around to see part two.

THE END

You and Lady Jaye enter the ballroom where the COBRA meeting is being held. COBRA Commander looks in your direction.

"No!" he shouts, pointing right at Lady Jaye. Your heart stops. "I will not tolerate lateness." Your heart starts again. Lady Jaye offers her excuses and COBRA Commander goes on. She pulled it off!

"This is an important day—one of the most important days in the history of COBRA!" COBRA Commander goes on. "By nightfall all the poltron gas will be headed for Mt. Terrapin. The U.S. government thinks we don't know about their secret missile base. But they're wrong. We know about it. And soon we will own it!"

"What about The One?" asks Destro.

"He won't live to see tomorrow! Come, my dear Baroness," COBRA Commander says to Lady Jaye. "Let's go to the docks and watch our precious cargo as it's loaded."

What a disaster! COBRA is going to use poltron to overpower the forces protecting the base at Mt. Terrapin. The thought of these missiles in COBRA's hands—it's too awful for words! You've got to radio HQ. But how can you leave Lady Jaye alone with COBRA Commander? Quick, make a decision!

....

If you want to follow Lady Jaye and COBRA, turn to page 40.

If you want to slip away and radio the rest of the Team, turn to page 35.

78

You decide to use your martial-arts training.

Aieeah! Your left foot springs up and kicks the gun out of Bulldog's hand. Then you ram your elbow into his midsection. Not graceful. Not classic. But it works.

Bulldog doubles over in pain and you *run*! Past the commuters, around the ticket booths, past the line of people buying chocolate chip cookies, you run! You don't look back. Is he following? You can't think about that now. You just keep running past the shops and through the arch that leads to the subway.

Quick! Turn to page 64.

You reach the runway just as the COBRAS open fire. The roar of their weapons shakes the small landing strip, the sound echoing off the mountain peaks.

The plane cruises slowly across the runway. You run after it. You are almost up to it. A hand reaches out from the hatch door. You leap—the longest leap of your life—and grab the hand. Gung-Ho pulls you up into the cabin.

"Made it!" you cry.

"And I've made radio contact with HQ," Duke calls from the cockpit. "They've got the information they need to proceed. We didn't exactly wrap up everything in a neat package for them—but they want us stateside now."

"I still think we could've taken those CO-BRAS," Gung-Ho grumbles, as the plane lifts off and roars out of the range of the COBRAS' weapons. "Ain't I right?"

"Well...we probably would've gotten in your way," you say. "If you'd been on your own, you probably could've taken 'em!"

Even Gung-Ho has a good laugh at that one (even though he secretly agrees), and the flight back to HQ is a safe and happy one.

THE END

"I got a feel for this place when they were shoving me down here," Quick Kick says. "This is a real toughy."

"Do you still have all your gear? Can we bust out?"

"Sure. Even if I didn't, we could blow this place anyway." Quick Kick tests the bars. "Humph," he says. "Kid stuff."

"Then let's go!" you urge, not wanting to hang around any longer than necessary.

"Hold on a minute, my friend. Maybe we shouldn't be so hasty. We could bust out now and take our chances. Or we could rest up a bit and devise a foolproof plan. Or we could stay and let them make the first move. Then we can learn what COBRA's up to here. If we split now, this mission is a wash."

....

If you decide you can't stand this cell another second, turn to page 72.

If you decide haste makes waste and you'd better plan your getaway, turn to page 22.

If you decide to see what tricks COBRA's up to, turn to page 60.

82

You run to the right—right into a platoon of COBRA guards! You slash your laser knife to the right, to the left. *KABOOM!* Two guards hit the floor. *KERPLOW!* Quick Kick's hands and feet move faster than your eye.

But finally the sheer number of COBRA guards beats you down.

You and Quick Kick are bound and gagged, then blindfolded. Oh no, not again.

Yes, again. Up and down endless halls and ramps. You're sweating at the pace. But you cool off quickly as you're jerked outside and dumped into the back of a van.

"Sorry," you say as you bounce against Quick Kick. The van is bouncing over rough, winding roads.

"Not as sorry as you're going to be," says a raspy voice.

Suddenly the van slams to a halt. The door opens and a breeze hits you. It smells of the sea.

"You know the saying, 'Up a creek without a paddle'?" the raspy voice asks. "Well, this is in the ocean without a boat, but with a few lead weights. Let's see you swim out of this one." *SPLASH!* As the water closes over your head, you know for sure that this is...

THE END

After what seems like half an hour, there are no more stops and starts. You must be in the country. You hear a train whistle in the distance. Then the road begins to curve. You get jounced back and forth against Bulldog.

"Excuse me," you say. He says nothing. Then the car slows.

"Mrrrumph," the driver says, probably into a receiver.

Crrreeeaaakkkk. A gate opens.

Something scratches across the roof of the car as it creeps forward.

You hear a garage door open and the car stops. Your door opens. You are roughly pulled out, then pushed into an elevator.

You drop down, down in total blindness. Your stomach feels as if it's on the top of the elevator car.

Clunk. The elevator stops and you're shoved off. You fall on your knees. *Crunch*. It hurts even worse than it sounds. You realize that you're all alone, kneeling on the floor. Around you is nothing but darkness and silence.

And then, from far away, come footsteps. Slow and steady as if they know where they're going and what they're going to do.

....
Turn to page 30.

You stay crouched down behind the pizza counter. The man who's following you might still be out there waiting. The pizza man keeps singing. Luckily, he has a nice voice.

After about ten minutes, you call "*Ciao*" to him, slip out from behind the counter, and head for the waiting room.

Bulldog is nowhere in sight.

But someone else is—wearing a white karate outfit, has black belt, and a stern expression on his handsome Oriental face. It's Quick Kick. Even in the strange crowd that hangs around in the station, he stands out.

"Hey, man," he greets you. "Been here long?"

You explain about Bulldog and the pizza stand.

"Don't worry," he says. "Our train leaves in ten minutes, and there are no animals allowed."

"But he's not really..." you begin.

"Don't sweat it, man. You're in good hands—and feet—with Quick Kick."

You hope he's right.

As you board the train, you catch a glimpse of a guy in a dark green coat and sunglasses. You freeze. But it's just another dog-tired end-of-the-day commuter.

Turn to page 12.

Gung-Ho has a lot of fine qualities. As a bare-knuckle brawler and a fighting Marine, there's no one better.

But let's face it, as a military strategist, Gung-Ho leaves a lot to be desired. In fact, if you listen to him and charge in no matter what the odds are against you, chances are you'll get your head blown off.

Which—guess what?—is just what happens.

Maybe next time you'll let a cooler head prevail and head off in a wiser—and safer—direction!

THE END

"Well, that's all very interesting," you say, "but what about Gung-Ho? Isn't there something we can do for him?"

The One smiles slyly. "I alone have the antidote to poltron. I could give it to you...if you promise to clear out—permanently."

"Yeah, and what are you going to do about COBRA breathing down your neck?" asks Duke. "You're not calling the shots anymore!"

"Oh, I forgot." The One's shoulders droop.

"Look, give us the antidote," says Duke. "You get your life. We get the poltron mines out of COBRA's mitts. And as a bonus, you get a one-way ticket to Tahiti."

"But then I have to give up Kamali, my kingdom," The One says.

"Well, you can't have everything," says Duke. "And with COBRA, it's not going to be white beaches and soft breezes. Deal?"

The One knows he has no choice.

"Don't take it too hard," says Duke. "After all, not everybody gets to be a king. At least you have your memories."

THE END

When Duke and Gung-Ho and the rest are finished slapping you on the back and congratulating you, you tell them the whole incredible story.

"Looks like we have to pay a visit to The One back at the palace," says Duke.

Outfitted with gas masks and spraying a cloud of poltron in front of you, you take the palace with ease. You find the quivering ex-ruler waiting at your mercy.

"Just don't torture me," he pleads.

You can now close the chapter on Kamali.

Later, you learn that the United Nations will take over the poltron mines and the processing plant. Kamali will be returned to Mombania.

As for The One, after seeing what COBRA had in store for him, he's almost glad to remain in custody.

"It's going to be a long time before he gets back to the Bronx," Duke says. And everyone laughs.

Your eyes go from one happy face to another. Your smile is the broadest. You made it, Joe. You're really part of the team. Mission accomplished!

THE END